Marx Joyce
Hardy Chesterton Austen
Defoe Abbott Cooper Emerson Hugo
Melville Montaigne Machiavelli Eliot Grimm
Stoker Christie Haggard Molière
Wilde Carroll Maupassant Byron Schiller
Garnett Engels
Goethe Fitzgerald Hawthorne Smith Kafka
Cotton Einstein Dostoyevsky Hall
Baum Kipling Doyle Willis
Henry Nietzsche
Leslie Dumas Flaubert Turgenev Balzac
Stockton Vatsyayana Crane
Burroughs Verne
Curtis Tocqueville Gogol Vinci
Homer Widger Tolstoy Whitman Busch
Darwin Thoreau Twain Scott
Potter Freud Zola Lawrence Plato Harte
Kant Jowett Stevenson Dickens Burton Hesse
Andersen Cervantes
London Descartes Voltaire
Poe Aristotle Wells
Hale James Hastings Cooke
Bunner Shakespeare Irving
Richter Chambers da Shaw Alcott
Doré Dante Chekhov Wodehouse Benedict
Swift Pushkin
Newton

tredition®

tredition was established in 2006 by Sandra Latusseck and Soenke Schulz. Based in Hamburg, Germany, tredition offers publishing solutions to authors and publishing houses, combined with world-wide distribution of printed and digital book content. tredition is uniquely positioned to enable authors and publishing houses to create books on their own terms and without conventional manu-facturing risks.

For more information please visit: www.tredition.com

TREDITION CLASSICS

This book is part of the TREDITION CLASSICS series. The creators of this series are united by passion for literature and driven by the intention of making all public domain books available in printed format again - worldwide. Most TREDITION CLASSICS titles have been out of print and off the bookstore shelves for decades. At tredi-tion we believe that a great book never goes out of style and that its value is eternal. Several mostly non-profit literature projects pro-vide content to tredition. To support their good work, tredition donates a portion of the proceeds from each sold copy. As a reader of a TREDITION CLASSICS book, you support our mission to save many of the amazing works of world literature from oblivion. See all available books at www.tredition.com.

 Project Gutenberg

The content for this book has been graciously provided by Project Gutenberg. Project Gutenberg is a non-profit organization founded by Michael Hart in 1971 at the University of Illinois. The mission of Project Gutenberg is simple: To encourage the creation and distribu-tion of eBooks. Project Gutenberg is the first and largest collection of public domain eBooks.

Ernest Maltravers

Volume 6

Baron Edward Bulwer Lytton Lytton

Imprint

This book is part of TREDITION CLASSICS

Author: Baron Edward Bulwer Lytton Lytton
Cover design: Buchgut, Berlin – Germany

Publisher: tredition GmbH, Hamburg - Germany
ISBN: 978-3-8424-3088-4

www.tredition.com
www.tredition.de

BOOK VI.

Perchance you say that gold's the arch-exceller,
And to be rich is sweet?—EURIP. /Ion./, line 641.

* * * 'Tis not to be endured,
To yield our trodden path and turn aside,
Giving our place to knaves.—/Ibid./, line 648

CHAPTER I.

"L'adresse et l'artifice out passe dans mon coeur;
Qu'ou a sous cet habit et d'esprit et de ruse."*—REGNARD.

* Subtility and craft have taken possession of my heart; but under this habit one exhibits both shrewdness and wit.

IT was a fine morning in July, when a gentleman who had arrived in town the night before—after an absence from England of several years—walked slowly and musingly up the superb thoroughfare which connects the Regent's park with St. James's.

He was a man, who, with great powers of mind, had wasted his youth in a wandering vagabond kind of life, but who had worn away the love of pleasure, and began to awaken to a sense of ambition.

"It is astonishing how this city is improved," said he to himself. "Everything gets on in this world with a little energy and bustle—and everybody as well as everything. My old cronies, fellows not half so clever as I am, are all doing well. There's Tom Stevens, my very fag at Eton—snivelling little dog he was too!—just made under-secretary of state. Pearson, whose longs and shorts I always wrote, is now head-master to the human longs and shorts of a public school—editing Greek plays, and booked for a bishopric. Collier, I see by the papers, is leading his circuit—and Ernest Maltravers (but /he/ had some talent) has made a name in the world. Here am I, worth them all put together, who have done nothing but spend half my little fortune in spite of all my economy. Egad, this must have an end. I must look to the main chance; and yet, just when I want his help the most, my worthy uncle thinks fit to marry again. Humph—I'm too good for this world."

While thus musing, the soliloquist came in direct personal contact with a tall gentleman, who carried his head very high in the air, and did not appear to see that he had nearly thrown our abstracted philosopher off his legs.

"Zounds, sir, what do you mean?" cried the latter.

"I beg your par—" began the other, meekly, when his arm was seized, and the injured man exclaimed, "Bless me, sir, is it indeed /you/ whom I see?"

"Ha!—Lumley?"

"The same; and how fares it, any dear uncle? I did not know you were in
London. I only arrived last night. How well you are looking!"

"Why, yes, Heaven be praised, I am pretty well."

"And happy in your new ties? You must present me to Mrs. Templeton."

"Ehem," said Mr. Templeton, clearing his throat, and with a slight but embarrassed smile, "I never thought I should marry again."

"/L'homme propose et Dieu dispose/," observed Lumley Ferrers; for it was he.

"Gently, my dear nephew," replied Mr. Templeton, gravely; "those phrases are somewhat sacrilegious; I am an old-fashioned person, you know."

"Ten thousand apologies."

"/One/ apology will suffice; these hyperboles of phrase are almost sinful."

"Confounded old prig!" thought Ferrers; but he bowed sanctimoniously.

"My dear uncle, I have been a wild fellow in my day; but with years comes reflection; and under your guidance, if I may hope for it, I trust to grow a wiser and a better man."

"It is well, Lumley," returned the uncle, "and I am very glad to see you returned to your own country. Will you dine with me to-morrow? I am living near Fulham. You had better bring your carpet-bag, and stay with me some days; you will be heartily welcome, especially if you can shift without a foreign servant. I have a great compassion for papists, but—"

"Oh, my dear uncle, do not fear; I am not rich enough to have a foreign servant, and have not travelled over three-quarters of the globe without learning that it is possible to dispense with a valet."

"As to being rich enough," observed Mr. Templeton, with a calculating air, "seven hundred and ninety-five pounds ten shillings a year will allow a man to keep two servants, if he pleases; but I am glad to find you economical at all events. We meet to-morrow, then, at six o'clock."

"/Au revoir/—I mean, God bless you.

"Tiresome old gentleman that," muttered Ferrers, "and not so cordial as formerly; perhaps his wife is /enceinte/, and he is going to do me the injustice of having another heir. I must look to this; for without riches, I had better go back and live /au cinquieme/ at Paris."

With this conclusion, Lumley quickened his pace, and soon arrived at Seamore Place. In a few moments more he was in the library well stored with books, and decorated with marble busts and images from the studios of Canova and Thorwaldsen.

"My master, sir, will be down immediately," said the servant who admitted him; and Ferrers threw himself on a sofa, and contemplated the apartment with an air half envious and half cynical.

Presently the door opened, and "My dear Ferrers!" "Well, /mon cher/, how are you?" were the salutations hastily exchanged.

After the first sentences of inquiry, gratulation, and welcome, had cleared the way for more general conversation,—"Well, Maltravers," said Ferrers, "so here we are together again, and after a lapse of so many years! both older, certainly; and you, I suppose, wiser. At all events, people think you so; and that's all that's important in the question. Why, man, you are looking as young as ever, only a little paler and thinner; but look at me—I am not very /much/ past thirty, and I am almost an old man; bald at the temples, crows' feet, too, eh! Idleness ages one damnably."

"Pooh, Lumley, I never saw you look better. And are you really come to settle in England?"

"Yes, if I can afford it. But at my age, and after having seen so much, the life of an idle, obscure /garcon/ does not content me. I feel that the world's opinion, which I used to despise, is growing necessary to me. I want to be something. What can I be? Don't look alarmed, I won't rival you. I dare say literary reputation is a fine thing, but I desire some distinction more substantial and worldly. You know your own country; give me a map of the roads to Power."

"To Power! Oh, nothing but law, politics, and riches."

"For law I am too old; politics, perhaps, might suit me; but riches, my dear Ernest—ah, how I long for a good account with my banker!"

"Well, patience and hope. Are you are not a rich uncle's heir?"

"I don't know," said Ferrers, very dolorously; "the old gentleman has married again, and may have a family."

"Married!—to whom?"

"A widow, I hear; I know nothing more, except that she has a child already. So you see she has got into a cursed way of having children. And perhaps, by the time I'm forty, I shall see a whole covey of cherubs flying away with the great Templeton property!"

"Ha, ha; your despair sharpens your wit, Lumley; but why not take a leaf out of your uncle's book, and marry yourself?"

"So I will when I can find an heiress. If that is what you meant to say—it is a more sensible suggestion than any I could have supposed to come from a man who writes books, especially poetry: and your advice is not to be despised. For rich I will be; and as the fathers (I don't mean of the Church, but in Horace) told the rising generation, the first thing is to resolve to be rich, it is only the second thing to consider how."

"Meanwhile, Ferrers, you will be my guest."

"I'll dine with you to-day; but to-morrow I am off to Fulham, to be introduced to my aunt. Can't you fancy her?—grey /gros-de-Naples/ gown: gold chain with an eyeglass; rather fat; two pugs, and a parrot! 'Start not, this is fancy's sketch!' I have not yet seen the respectable relative with my physical optics. What shall we have for dinner? Let me choose, you were always a bad caterer." As Ferrers thus rattled on, Maltravers felt himself growing younger: old times and old adventures crowded fast upon him; and the two friends spent a most agreeable day together. It was only the next morning that Maltravers, in thinking over the various conversations that had passed between them, was forced reluctantly to acknowledge that the inert selfishness of Lumley Ferrers seemed now to have hardened into a resolute and systematic want of principle, which might, perhaps, make him a dangerous and designing man, if urged by circumstances into action.

CHAPTER II.

"/Dauph./ Sir, I must speak to you. I have been long your despised kinsman.

"/Morose./ Oh, what thou wilt, nephew."—EPICENE.

"Her silence is dowry eno'—exceedingly soft spoken; thrifty of her speech, that spends but six words a day."—/Ibid./

THE coach dropped Mr. Ferrers at the gate of a villa about three miles from town. The lodge-keeper charged himself with the carpet-bag, and Ferrers strolled, with his hands behind him (it was his favourite mode of disposing of them), through the beautiful and elaborate pleasure-grounds.

"A very nice, snug little box (jointure-house, I suppose)! I would not grudge that, I'm sure, if I had but the rest. But here, I suspect, comes madam's first specimen of the art of having a family." This last thought was extracted from Mr. Ferrers's contemplative brain by a lovely little girl, who came running up to him, fearless and spoilt as she was; and, after indulging a tolerable stare, exclaimed, "Are you come to see papa, sir?"

"Papa!—the deuce!"—thought Lumley; "and who is papa, my dear?"

"Why, mamma's husband. He is not my papa by rights."

"Certainly not, my love; not by rights—I comprehend."

"Eh!"

"Yes, I am going to see your papa by wrongs—Mr. Templeton."

"Oh, this way, then."

"You are very fond of Mr. Templeton, my little angel."

"To be sure I am. You have not seen the rocking-horse he is going to give me."

"Not yet, sweet child! And how is mamma?"

"Oh, poor, dear mamma," said the child, with a sudden change of voice, and tears in her eyes. "Ah, she is not well!"

"In the family way, to a dead certainty!" muttered Ferrers with a groan: "but here is my uncle. Horrid name! Uncles were always wicked fellows. Richard the Third and the man who did something or other to the babes in the wood were a joke to my hard-hearted old relation, who has robbed me with a widow! The lustful, liquor-ish old—My /dear/ sir, I'm so glad to see you!"

Mr. Templeton, who was a man very cold in his manners, and always either looked over people's heads or down upon the ground, just touched his nephew's outstretched hand, and telling him he was welcome, observed that it was a very fine afternoon.

"Very, indeed; sweet place this; you see, by the way, that I have already made acquaintance with my fair cousin-in-law. She is very pretty."

"I really think she is," said Mr. Templeton, with some warmth, and gazing fondly at the child, who was now throwing buttercups up in the air, and trying to catch them. Mr. Ferrers wished in his heart that they had been brickbats!

"Is she like her mother?" asked the nephew.

"Like whom, sir?"

"Her mother—Mrs. Templeton."

"No, not very; there is an air, perhaps, but the likeness is not re-markably strong. Would you not like to go to your room before dinner?"

"Thank you. Can I not first be presented to Mrs. Tem—"

"She is at her devotions, Mr. Lumley," interrupted Mr. Templeton, grimly.

"The she-hypocrite!" thought Ferrers. "Oh, I am delighted that your pious heart has found so congenial a helpmate!"

"It is a great blessing, and I am grateful for it. This is the way to the house."

Lumley, now formally installed in a grave bedroom, with dimity curtains and dark-brown paper with light-brown stars on it, threw himself into a large chair, and yawned and stretched with as much fervour as if he could have yawned and stretched himself into his uncle's property. He then slowly exchanged his morning dress for a quiet suit of black, and thanked his stars that, amidst all his sins, he had never been a dandy, and had never rejoiced in a fine waist-coat — a criminal possession that he well knew would have entirely hardened his uncle's conscience against him. He tarried in his room till the second bell summoned him to descend; and then, entering the drawing-room, which had a cold look even in July, found his uncle standing by the mantelpiece, and a young, slight, handsome woman, half-buried in a huge but not comfortable /fauteuil/.

"Your aunt, Mrs. Templeton; madam, my nephew, Mr. Lumley Ferrers," said
Templeton, with a wave of the hand.

"John, — dinner!"

"I hope I am not late!"

"No," said Templeton, gently, for he had always liked his nephew, and began now to thaw towards him a little on seeing that Lumley put a good face upon the new state of affairs.

"No, my dear boy — no; but I think order and punctuality cardinal virtues in a well-regulated family."

"Dinner, sir," said the butler, opening the folding-doors at the end of the room.

"Permit me," said Lumley, offering his arm to his aunt. "What a lovely place this is!"

Mrs. Templeton said something in reply, but what it was Ferrers could not discover, so low and choked was the voice.

"Shy," thought he: "odd for a widow! but that's the way those husband-buriers take us in!"

Plain as was the general furniture of the apartment, the natural ostentation of Mr. Templeton broke out in the massive value of the plate, and the number of the attendants. He was a rich man, and he was proud of his riches: he knew it was respectable to be rich, and he thought it was moral to be respectable. As for the dinner, Lumley knew enough of his uncle's tastes to be prepared for viands and wines that even he (fastidious gourmand as he was) did not despise.

Between the intervals of eating, Mr. Ferrers endeavoured to draw his aunt into conversation, but he found all his ingenuity fail him. There was, in the features of Mrs. Templeton, an expression of deep but calm melancholy, that would have saddened most persons to look upon, especially in one so young and lovely. It was evidently something beyond shyness or reserve that made her so silent and subdued, and even in her silence there was so much natural sweetness, that Ferrers could not ascribe her manner to haughtiness or the desire to repel. He was rather puzzled; "for though," thought he, sensibly enough, "my uncle is not a youth, he is a very rich fellow; and how any widow, who is married again to a rich old fellow, can be melancholy, passes my understanding!"

Templeton, as if to draw attention from his wife's taciturnity, talked more than usual. He entered largely into politics, and regretted that in times so critical he was not in parliament.

"Did I possess your youth and your health, Lumley, I would not neglect my country—Popery is abroad."

"I myself should like very much to be in parliament," said Lumley, boldly.

"I dare say you would," returned the uncle, drily. "Parliament is very expensive—only fit for those who have a large stake in the country. Champagne to Mr. Ferrers."

Lumley bit his lip, and spoke little during the rest of the dinner. Mr. Templeton, however, waxed gracious by the time the dessert was on the table; and began cutting up a pineapple, with many assurances to Lumley that gardens were nothing without pineries. "Whenever you settle in the country, nephew, be sure you have a pinery."

"Oh, yes," said Lumley, almost bitterly, "and a pack of hounds, and a
French cook; they will all suit my fortune very well."

"You are more thoughtful on pecuniary matters than you used to be," said the uncle.

"Sir," replied Ferrers, solemnly, "in a very short time I shall be what is called a middle-aged man."

"Humph!" said the host.

There was another silence. Lumley was a man, as we have said, or implied before, of great knowledge of human nature, at least the ordinary sort of it, and he now revolved in his mind the various courses it might be wise to pursue towards his rich relation. He saw that, in delicate fencing, his uncle had over him the same advantage that a tall man has over a short one with the physical sword-play;— by holding his weapon in a proper position, he kept the other at arm's length. There was a grand reserve and dignity about the man who had something to give away, of which Ferrers, however actively he might shift his ground and flourish his rapier, could not break the defence. He determined, therefore, upon a new game, for which his frankness of manner admirably adapted him. Just as he formed this resolution, Mrs. Templeton rose, and with a gentle bow, and soft though languid smile, glided from the room. The two gentlemen resettled themselves, and Templeton pushed the bottle to Ferrers.

"Help yourself, Lumley! your travels seem to have deprived you of your high spirits—you are pensive."

"Sir," said Ferrers, abruptly, "I wish to consult you."

"Oh, young man! you have been guilty of some excess—you have gambled—you have—"

"I have done nothing, sir, that should make me less worthy your esteem. I repeat, I wish to consult you; I have outlived the hot days of my youth—I am now alive to the claims of the world. I have talents, I believe; and I have application, I know. I wish to fill a position in the world that may redeem my past indolence, and do credit to my family. Sir, I set your example before me, and I now ask your counsel, with the determination to follow it."

Templeton was startled; he half shaded his face with his hand, and gazed searchingly upon the high forehead and bold eyes of his nephew. "I believe you are sincere," said he, after a pause.

"You may well believe so, sir."

"Well, I will think of this. I like an honourable ambition—not too extravagant a one,—/that/ is sinful; but a /respectable/ station in the world is a proper object of desire, and wealth is a blessing; because," added the rich man, taking another slice of the pineapple,— "it enables us to be of use to our fellow-creatures!"

"Sir, then," said Ferrers, with daring animation—"then I avow that my ambition is precisely of the kind you speak of. I am obscure, I desire to be reputably known; my fortune is mediocre, I desire it to be great. I ask you for nothing—I know your generous heart; but I wish independently to work out my own career."

"Lumley," said Templeton, "I never esteemed you so much as I do now. Listen to me—I will confide in you; I think the government are under obligations to me."

"I know it," exclaimed Ferrers, whose eyes sparkled at the thought of a sinecure—for sinecures then existed!

"And," pursued the uncle, "I intend to ask them a favour in return."

"Oh, sir!"

"Yes; I think—mark me—with management and address, I may—"

"Well, my dear sir!"

"Obtain a barony for myself and heirs; I trust I shall soon have a family!"

Had somebody given Lumley Ferrers a hearty cuff on the ear, he would have thought less of it than of this wind-up of his uncle's ambitious projects. His jaws fell, his eyes grew an inch larger, and he remained perfectly speechless.

"Ay," pursued Mr. Templeton, "I have long dreamed this; my character is spotless, my fortune great. I have ever exerted my parliamentary influence in favour of ministers; and, in this commercial country, no man has higher claims than Richard Templeton to the honours of a virtuous, loyal, and religious state. Yes, my boy, — I like your ambition — you see I have some of it myself; and since you are sincere in your wish to tread in my footsteps, I think I can obtain you a junior partnership in a highly respectable establishment. Let me see; your capital now is —

"Pardon me, sir," interrupted Lumley, colouring with indignation despite himself; "I honour commerce much, but my paternal relations are not such as would allow me to enter into trade. And permit me to add," continued he, seizing with instant adroitness the new weakness presented to him — "permit me to add, that those relations, who have been ever kind to me, would, properly managed, be highly efficient in promoting your own views of advancement; for your sake I would not break with them. Lord Saxingham is still a minister — nay, he is in the cabinet."

"Hem — Lumley — hem!" said Templeton, thoughtfully; "we will consider — we will consider. Any more wine?"

"No, I thank you, sir."

"Then I'll just take my evening stroll, and think over matters. You can rejoin Mrs. Templeton. And I say, Lumley, — I read prayers at nine o'clock. Never forget your Maker, and He will not forget you. The barony will be an excellent thing — eh? — an English peerage — yes — an English peerage! very different from your beggarly countships abroad!"

So saying, Mr. Templeton rang for his hat and cane, and stepped into the lawn from the window of the dining-room.

"'The world's mine oyster, which I with sword will open,'" muttered Ferrers; "I would mould this selfish old man to my purpose; for, since I have neither genius to write nor eloquence to declaim, I will at least see whether I have not cunning to plot and courage to act. Conduct — conduct — conduct — there lies my talent; and what is conduct but a steady walk from a design to its execution?"

With these thoughts Ferrers sought Mrs. Templeton. He opened the folding-doors very gently, for all his habitual movements were quick and noiseless, and perceived that Mrs. Templeton sat by the window, and that she seemed engrossed with a book which lay open on a little work-table before her.

"Fordyce's /Advice to Young Married Women/, I suppose. Sly jade! However, I must not have her against me."

He approached; still Mrs. Templeton did not note him; nor was it till he stood facing her that he himself observed that her tears were falling fast over the page.

He was a little embarrassed, and, turning towards the window, affected to cough, and then said, without looking at Mrs. Templeton, "I fear I have disturbed you."

"No," answered the same low, stifled voice that had before replied to Lumley's vain attempts to provoke conversation; "it was a melancholy employment, and perhaps it is not right to indulge in it."

"May I inquire what author so affected you."

"It is but a volume of poems, and I am no judge of poetry; but it contains thoughts which—which—" Mrs. Templeton paused abruptly, and Lumley quietly took up the book.

"Ah!" said he, turning to the title-page—"my friend ought to be much flattered."

"Your friend?"

"Yes: this, I see, is by Ernest Maltravers, a very intimate ally of mine."

"I should like to see him," cried Mrs. Templeton, almost with animation. "I read but little; it was by chance that I met with one of his books, and they are as if I heard a dear friend speaking to me. Ah! I should like to see him!"

"I'm sure, madam," said the voice of a third person, in an austere and rebuking accent, "I do not see what good it would do your immortal soul to see a man who writes idle verses, which appear to me, indeed, highly immoral. I just looked into that volume this morning and found nothing but trash—love-sonnets, and such stuff."

Mrs. Templeton made no reply, and Lumley, in order to change the conversation, which seemed a little too matrimonial for his taste, said, rather awkwardly, "You are returned very soon, sir."

"Yes, I don't like walking in the rain!"

"Bless me, it rains, so, it does—I had not observed—"

"Are you wet, sir? had you not better—" began the wife timidly.

"No, ma'am, I'm not wet, I thank you. By the by, nephew, this new author is a friend of yours. I wonder a man of his family should condescend to turn author. He can come to no good. I hope you will drop his acquaintance—authors are very unprofitable associates, I'm sure. I trust I shall see no more of Mr. Maltravers's books in my house."

"Nevertheless, he is well thought of, sir, and makes no mean figure in the world," said Lumley, stoutly; for he was by no means disposed to give up a friend who might be as useful to him as Mr. Templeton himself.

"Figure or no figure—I have not had many dealings with authors in my day; and when I had I always repented it. Not sound, sir, not sound—all cracked somewhere. Mrs. Templeton, have the kindness to get the Prayer-book—my hassock must be fresh stuffed, it gives me quite a pain in my knee. Lumley, will you ring the bell? Your aunt is very melancholy. True religion is not gloomy; we will read a sermon on Cheerfulness."

"So, so," said Mr. Ferrers to himself, as he undressed that night— "I see that my uncle is a little displeased with my aunt's pensive face—a little jealous of her thinking of anything but himself: /tant mieux/. I must work upon this discovery; it will not do for them to live too happily with each other. And what with that lever, and what with his ambitious projects, I think I see a way to push the good things of this world a few inches nearer to Lumley Ferrers."

CHAPTER III.

"The pride too of her step, as light
 Along the unconscious earth she went,
 Seemed that of one born with a right
 To walk some heavenlier element."
            /Loves of the Angels./

    "Can it be
That these fine impulses, these lofty thoughts
Burning with their own beauty, are but given
To make me the low slave of vanity?"—/Erinna./

    "Is she not too fair
Even to think of maiden's sweetest care?
The mouth and brow are contrasts."—/Ibid./

IT was two or three evenings after the date of the last chapter, and there was what the newspapers call "a select party" in one of the noblest mansions in London. A young lady, on whom all eyes were bent, and whose beauty might have served the painter for a model of Semiramis or Zenobia, more majestic than became her years, and so classically faultless as to have something cold and statue-like in its haughty lineaments, was moving through the crowd that murmured applauses as she passed. This lady was Florence Lascelles, the daughter of Lumley's great relation, the Earl of Saxingham, and supposed to be the richest heiress in England. Lord Saxingham himself drew aside his daughter as she swept along.

"Florence," said he in a whisper, "the Duke of — — — is greatly struck with you—be civil to him—I am about to present him."

So saying, the earl turned to a small, dark, stiff-looking man, of about twenty-eight years of age, at his left, and introduced the Duke of — — — to Lady Florence Lascelles. The duke was unmarried; it was an introduction between the greatest match and the wealthiest heiress in the peerage.

"Lady Florence," said Lord Saxingham, "is as fond of horses as yourself, duke, though not quite so good a judge."

"I confess I /do/ like horses," said the duke, with an ingenuous air.

Lord Saxingham moved away.

Lady Florence stood mute—one glance of bright contempt shot from her large eyes; her lip slightly curled, and she then half turned aside, and seemed to forget that her new acquaintance was in existence.

His grace, like most great personages, was not apt to take offence; nor could he, indeed, ever suppose that any slight towards the Duke of — — — could be intended; still he thought it would be proper in Lady Florence to begin the conversation; for he himself, though not shy, was habitually silent, and accustomed to be saved the fatigue of defraying the small charges of society. After a pause, seeing, however, that Lady Florence remained speechless, he began:

"You ride sometimes in the Park, Lady Florence?"

"Very seldom."

"It is, indeed, too warm for riding at present."

"I did not say so."

"Hem—I thought you did."

Another pause.

"Did you speak, Lady Florence?"

"No."

"Oh, I beg pardon—Lord Saxingham is looking very well."

"I am glad you think so."

"Your picture in the exhibition scarcely does you justice, Lady Florence; yet Lawrence is usually happy."

"You are very flattering," said Lady Florence, with a lively and perceptible impatience in her tone and manner. The young beauty was thoroughly spoilt—and now all the scorn of a scornful nature was drawn forth, by observing the envious eyes of the crowd were bent upon one whom the Duke of — — — was actually talking to. Brilliant as were her own powers of conversation, she would not deign to exert them—she was an aristocrat of intellect rather than birth, and she took it into her head that the duke was an idiot. She was very much mistaken. If she had but broken up the ice, she would have found that the water below was not shallow. The duke, in fact, like many other Englishmen, though he did not like the trouble of showing forth, and had an ungainly manner, was a man who had read a good deal, possessed a sound head and an honourable mind, though he did not know what it was to love anybody, to care much for anything, and was at once perfectly sated and yet perfectly contented; for apathy is the combination of satiety and content.

Still Florence judged of him as lively persons are apt to judge of the sedate; besides, she wanted to proclaim to him and to everybody else, how little she cared for dukes and great matches; she, therefore, with a slight inclination of her head, turned away, and extended her hand to a dark young man, who was gazing on her with that respectful but unmistakable admiration which proud women are never proud enough to despise.

"Ah, signor," said she, in Italian, "I am so glad to see you; it is a relief, indeed, to find genius in a crowd of nothings."

So saying, the heiress seated herself on one of those convenient couches which hold but two, and beckoned the Italian to her side. Oh, how the vain heart of Castruccio Cesarini beat!—what visions of love, rank, wealth, already flitted before him!

"I almost fancy," said Castruccio, "that the old days of romance are returned, when a queen could turn from princes and warriors to listen to a troubadour."

"Troubadours are now more rare than warriors and princes," replied Florence, with gay animation, which contrasted strongly with the coldness she had manifested to the Duke of — — —, "and therefore it would not now be a very great merit in a queen to fly from dulness and insipidity to poetry and wit."

"Ah, say not wit," said Cesarini; "wit is incompatible with the grave character of deep feelings;—incompatible with enthusiasm, with worship;—incompatible with the thoughts that wait upon Lady Florence Lascelles."

Florence coloured and slightly frowned; but the immense distinction between her position and that of the young foreigner, with her own inexperience, both of real life and the presumption of vain hearts, made her presently forget the flattery that would have offended her in another. She turned the conversation, however, into general channels, and she talked of Italian poetry with a warmth and eloquence worthy of the theme. While they thus conversed, a new guest had arrived, who, from the spot where he stood, engaged with Lord Saxingham, fixed a steady and scrutinising gaze upon the pair.

"Lady Florence has indeed improved," said this new guest. "I could not have conceived that England boasted any one half so beautiful."

"She certainly is handsome, my dear Lumley,—the Lascelles cast of countenance," replied Lord Saxingham," and so gifted! She is positively learned—quite a /bas bleu/. I tremble to think of the crowd of poets and painters who will make a fortune out of her enthusiasm. /Entre nous/, Lumley, I could wish her married to a man of sober sense, like the Duke of — — —; for sober sense is exactly what she wants. Do observe, she has been sitting just half an hour flirting with that odd-looking adventurer, a Signor Cesarini, merely because he writes sonnets and wears a dress like a stage-player!"

"It is the weakness of the sex, my dear lord," said Lumley; "they like to patronise, and they dote upon all oddities, from China monsters to cracked poets. But I fancy, by a restless glance cast every now and then around the room, that my beautiful cousin has in her something of the coquette."

"There you are quite right, Lumley," returned Lord Saxingham, laughing; "but I will not quarrel with her for breaking hearts and refusing hands, if she do but grow steady at last, and settle into the Duchess of − − −."

"Duchess of − − −!" repeated Lumley, absently; "well, I will go and present myself. I see she is growing tired of the signor. I will sound her as to the ducal impressions, my dear lord."

"Do−I dare not," replied the father; "she is an excellent girl, but heiresses are always contradictory. It was very foolish to deprive me of all control over her fortune. Come and see me again soon, Lumley. I suppose you are going abroad?"

"No, I shall settle in England; but of my prospects and plans more hereafter."

With this, Lumley quietly glided away to Florence. There was something in Ferrers that was remarkable from its very simplicity. His clear, sharp features, with the short hair and high brow−the absolute plainness of his dress, and the noiseless, easy, self-collected calm of all his motions, made a strong contrast to the showy Italian, by whose side he now stood. Florence looked up at him with some little surprise at his intrusion.

"Ah, you don't recollect me!" said Lumley, with his pleasant laugh. "Faithless Imogen, after all your vows of constancy! Behold your Alonzo!

'The worms they crept in and the worms they crept out.'

"Don't you remember how you trembled when I told you that true story, as we

'Conversed as we sat on the green"?

"Oh!" cried Florence, "it is indeed you, my dear cousin−my dear Lumley!
What an age since we parted!"

"Don't talk of age−it is an ugly word to a man of my years. Pardon, signor, if I disturb you."

And here Lumley, with a low bow, slid coolly into the place which Cesarini, who had shyly risen, left vacant for him. Castruccio looked disconcerted; but Florence had forgotten him in her delight at seeing Lumley, and Cesarini moved discontentedly away, and seated himself at a distance.

"And I come back," continued Lumley, "to find you a confirmed beauty and a professional coquette—don't blush!"

"Do they, indeed, call me a coquette?"

"Oh, yes,—for once the world is just."

"Perhaps I do deserve the reproach. Oh, Lumley, how I despise all that
I see and hear!"

"What, even the Duke of — — —?"

"Yes, I fear even the Duke of — — — is no exception!"

"Your father will go mad if he hear you."

"My father!—my poor father!—yes, he thinks the utmost that I, Florence Lascelles, am made for, is to wear a ducal coronet, and give the best balls in London."

"And pray what was Florence Lascelles made for?"

"Ah! I cannot answer the question. I fear for Discontent and Disdain."

"You are an enigma—but I will take pains and not rest till I solve you."

"I defy you."

"Thanks—better defy than despise.

"Oh, you must be strangely altered, if I can despise you."

"Indeed! what do you remember of me?"

"That you were frank, bold, and therefore, I suppose, true!—that you shocked my aunts and my father by your contempt for the vulgar hypocrisies of our conventional life. Oh, no! I cannot despise you."

Lumley raised his eyes to those of Florence—he gazed on her long and earnestly—ambitious hopes rose high within him.

"My fair cousin," said he, in an altered and serious tone, "I see something in your spirit kindred to mine; and I am glad that yours is one of the earliest voices which confirm my new resolves on my return to busy England!"

"And those resolves?"

"Are an Englishman's—energetic and ambitious."

"Alas, ambition! How many false portraits are there of the great original!"

Lumley thought he had found a clue to the heart of his cousin, and he began to expatiate, with unusual eloquence, on the nobleness of that daring sin which "lost angels heaven." Florence listened to him with attention, but not with sympathy. Lumley was deceived. His was not an ambition that could attract the fastidious but high-souled Idealist. The selfishness of his nature broke out in all the sentiments that he fancied would seem to her most elevated. Place—power—titles—all these objects were low and vulgar to one who saw them daily at her feet.

At a distance the Duke of — — — continued from time to time to direct his cold gaze at Florence. He did not like her the less for not seeming to court him. He had something generous within him, and could understand her. He went away at last, and thought seriously of Florence as a wife. Not a wife for companionship, for friendship, for love; but a wife who could take the trouble of rank off his hands—do him honour, and raise him an heir, whom he might flatter himself would be his own.

From his corner also, with dreams yet more vain and daring, Castruccio Cesarini cast his eyes upon the queen-like brow of the great heiress. Oh, yes, she had a soul—she could disdain rank and revere genius! What a triumph over De Montaigne—Maltravers—all the world, if he, the neglected poet, could win the hand for which the magnates of the earth sighed in vain! Pure and lofty as he thought himself, it was her birth and her wealth which Cesarini adored in Florence. And Lumley, nearer perhaps to the prize than either—yet still far off—went on conversing, with eloquent lips and sparkling eyes, while his cold heart was planning every word, dictating every glance, and laying out (for the most worldly are often the most visionary) the chart for a royal road to fortune. And Florence Lascelles, when the crowd had dispersed and she sought her chamber, forgot all three; and with that morbid romance often peculiar to those for whom Fate smiles the most, mused over the ideal image of the one she /could/ love—"in maiden meditation /not/ fancy-free!"

CHAPTER IV.

"In mea vesanas habui dispendia vires,
  Et valui poenas fortis in ipse meas."*—OVID.

  * I had the strength of a madman to my own cost, and employed that strength in my own punishment.

"Then might my breast be read within,
  A thousand volumes would be written there."
      EARL OF STIRLING.

ERNEST MALTRAVERS was at the height of his reputation; the work which he had deemed the crisis that was to make or mar him was the most brilliantly successful of all he had yet committed to the public. Certainly, chance did as much for it as merit, as is usually the case with works that become instantaneously popular. We may hammer away at the casket with strong arm and good purpose, and all in vain; when some morning a careless stroke hits the right nail on the head, and we secure the treasure.

It was at this time, when in the prime of youth—rich, courted, respected, run after—that Ernest Maltravers fell seriously ill. It was no active or visible disease, but a general irritability of the nerves, and a languid sinking of the whole frame. His labours began, perhaps, to tell against him. In earlier life he had been as active as a hunter of the chamois, and the hardy exercise of his frame counteracted the effects of a restless and ardent mind. The change from an athletic to a sedentary habit of life—the wear and tear of the brain—the absorbing passion for knowledge which day and night kept all his faculties in a stretch; made strange havoc in a constitution naturally strong. The poor author! how few persons understand; and forbear with, and pity him! He sells his health and youth to a rugged taskmaster. And, O blind and selfish world, you expect him to be as free of manner, and as pleasant of cheer, and as equal of mood, as if he were passing the most agreeable and healthful existence that pleasure could afford to smooth the wrinkles of the mind, or medicine invent to regulate the nerves of the body. But there was, besides all this, another cause that operated against the successful man!—His heart was too solitary. He lived without the sweet household ties—the connections and amities he formed excited for a moment, but possessed no charm to comfort or to soothe. Cleveland resided so much in the country, and was of so much calmer a temperament, and so much more advanced in age, that, with all the friendship that subsisted between them, there was none of that daily and familiar interchange of confidence which affectionate natures demand as the very food of life. Of his brother (as the reader will conjecture from never having been formally presented to him) Ernest saw but little. Colonel Maltravers, one of the gayest and handsomest men of his time, married a fine lady, lived principally at Paris, except when, for a few weeks in the shooting season, he filled his country house with companions who had nothing in common with Ernest: the brothers corresponded regularly every quarter, and saw each other once a year—this was all their intercourse. Ernest Maltravers stood in the world alone, with that cold but anxious spectre—Reputation.

It was late at night. Before a table covered with the monuments of erudition and thought sat a young man with a pale and worn countenance. The clock in the room told with a fretting distinctness every moment that lessened the journey to the grave. There was an anxious and expectant expression on the face of the student, and from time to time he glanced to the clock, and muttered to himself. Was it a letter from some adored mistress—the soothing flattery from some mighty arbiter of arts and letters—that the young man eagerly awaited? No; the aspirer was forgotten in the valetudinarian. Ernest Maltravers was waiting the visit of his physician, whom at that late hour a sudden thought had induced him to summon from his rest. At length the well-known knock was heard, and in a few moments the physician entered. He was one well versed in the peculiar pathology of book men, and kindly as well as skilful.

"My dear Mr. Maltravers, what is this? How are we?—not seriously ill, I hope—no relapse—pulse low and irregular, I see, but no fever. You are nervous."

"Doctor," said the student, "I did not send for you at this time of night from the idle fear or fretful caprice of an invalid. But when I saw you this morning, you dropped some hints which have haunted me ever since. Much that it befits the conscience and the soul to attend to without loss of time depends upon my full knowledge of my real state. If I understand you rightly, I may have but a short time to live—is it so?"

"Indeed!" said the doctor, turning away his face; "you have exaggerated my meaning. I did not say that you were in what we technically call danger."

"Am I then likely to be a /long/-lived man?"

The doctor coughed—"That is uncertain, my dear young friend," said he, after a pause.

"Be plain with me. The plans of life must be based upon such calculations as we can reasonably form of its probable duration. Do not fancy that I am weak enough or coward enough to shrink from any abyss which I have approached unconsciously; I desire—I adjure—nay, I command you to be explicit."

There was an earnest and solemn dignity in his patient's voice and manner which deeply touched and impressed the good physician.

"I will answer you frankly," said he; "you overwork the nerves and the brain; if you do not relax, you will subject yourself to confirmed disease and premature death. For several months—perhaps for years to come—you should wholly cease from literary labour. Is this a hard sentence? You are rich and young—enjoy yourself while you can."

Maltravers appeared satisfied—changed the conversation—talked easily on other matters for a few minutes: nor was it till he had dismissed his physician that he broke forth with the thoughts that were burning in him.

"Oh!" cried he aloud, as he rose and paced the room with rapid strides; "now, when I see before me the broad and luminous path, am I to be condemned to halt and turn aside? A vast empire rises on my view, greater than that of Caesars and conquerors—an empire durable and universal in the souls of men, that time itself cannot overthrow; and Death marches with me, side by side, and the skeleton hand waves me back to the nothingness of common men."

He paused at the casement—he threw it open, and leant forth and gasped for air. Heaven was serene and still, as morning came coldly forth amongst the waning stars; and the haunts of men, in their thoroughfare of idleness and of pleasure, were desolate and void. Nothing, save Nature, was awake.

"And if, O stars!" murmured Maltravers, from the depth of his excited heart—"if I have been insensible to your solemn beauty—if the Heaven and the Earth had been to me but as air and clay—if I were one of a dull and dim-eyed herd—I might live on, and drop into the grave from the ripeness of unprofitable years. It is because I yearn for the great objects of an immortal being, that life shrinks and shrivels up like a scroll. Away! I will not listen to these human and material monitors, and consider life as a thing greater than the things that I would live for. My choice is made, glory is more persuasive than the grave."

He turned impatiently from the casement—his eyes flashed—his chest heaved—he trod the chamber with a monarch's air. All the calculations of prudence, all the tame and methodical reasonings with which, from time to time, he had sought to sober down the impetuous man into the calm machine, faded away before the burst of awful and commanding passions that swept over his soul. Tell a man, in the full tide of his triumphs, that he bears death within him; and what crisis of thought can be more startling and more terrible!

Maltravers had, as we have seen, cared little for fame, till fame had been brought within his reach: then, with every step he took, new Alps had arisen. Each new conjecture brought to light a new truth that demanded enforcement or defence. Rivalry and competition chafed his blood, and kept his faculties at their full speed. He had the generous race-horse spirit of emulation. Ever in action, ever in progress, cheered on by the sarcasms of foes, even more than by the applause of friends, the desire of glory had become the habit of existence. When we have commenced a career, what stop is there till the grave?—where is the definite barrier of that ambition which, like the eastern bird, seems ever on the wing, and never rests upon the earth? Our names are not settled till our death: the ghosts of what we have done are made our haunting monitors — our scourging avengers — if ever we cease to do, or fall short of the younger past. Repose is oblivion; to pause is to unravel all the web that we have woven — until the tomb closes over us, and men, just when it is too late, strike the fair balance between ourselves and our rivals; and we are measured, not by the least, but by the greatest triumphs we have achieved. Oh, what a crushing sense of impotence comes over us, when we feel that our frame cannot support our mind — when the hand can no longer execute what the soul, actively as ever, conceives and desires! — the quick life tied to the dead form — the ideas fresh as immortality, gushing forth rich and golden, and the broken nerves, and the aching frame, and the weary eyes! — the spirit athirst for liberty and heaven — and the damning, choking consciousness that we are walled up and prisoned in a dungeon that must be our burial-place! Talk not of freedom — there is no such thing as freedom to a man whose body is the gaol, whose infirmities are the racks, of his genius!

Maltravers paused at last, and threw himself on his sofa, wearied and exhausted. Involuntarily, and as a half unconscious means of escaping from his conflicting and profitless emotions, he turned to several letters, which had for hours lain unopened on his table. Every one, the seal of which he broke, seemed to mock his state — every one seemed to attest the felicity of his fortunes. Some bespoke the admiring sympathy of the highest and wisest — one offered him a brilliant opening into public life — another (it was from Cleveland) was fraught with all the proud and rapturous approbation of a prophet whose auguries are at last fulfilled. At that letter Maltravers sighed deeply, and paused before he turned to the others. The last he opened was in an unknown hand, nor was any name affixed to it. Like all writers of some note, Maltravers was in the habit of receiving anonymous letters of praise, censure, warning, and exhortation — especially from young ladies at boarding schools, and old ladies in the country; but there was that in the first sentences of the letter, which he now opened with a careless hand, that riveted his attention. It was a small and beautiful handwriting, yet the letters were more clear and bold than they usually are in feminine caligraphy.

"Ernest Maltravers," began this singular effusion, "have you weighed yourself? Are you aware of your capacities? Do you feel that for you there may be a more dazzling reputation that that which appears to content you? You who seem to penetrate into the subtlest windings of the human heart, and to have examined nature as through a glass—you, whose thoughts stand forth like armies marshalled in defence of truth, bold and dauntless, and without a stain upon their glittering armour;—are you, at your age, and with your advantages, to bury yourself amidst books and scrolls? Do you forget that action is the grand career for men who think as you do? Will this word-weighing and picture-writing—the cold eulogies of pedants—the listless praises of literary idlers, content all the yearnings of your ambition? You were not made solely for the closet; 'The Dreams of Pindus, and the Aonian Maids' cannot endure through the noon of manhood. You are too practical for the mere poet, and too poetical to sink into the dull tenor of a learned life. I have never seen you, yet I know you—I read your spirit in your page; that aspiration for something better and greater than the great and the good, which colours all your passionate revelations of yourself and others—cannot be satisfied merely by ideal images. You cannot be contented, as poets and historians mostly are, by becoming great only from delineating great men, or imagining great events, or describing a great era. Is it not worthier of you to be what you fancy or relate? Awake, Maltravers, awake! Look into your heart, and feel your proper destinies. And who am I that thus address you?—a woman whose soul is filled with you—a woman in whom your eloquence has awakened, amidst frivolous and vain circles, the sense of a new existence—a woman who would make you, yourself, the embodied ideal of your own thoughts and dreams, and who would ask from earth no other lot than that of following you on the road of fame with the eyes of her heart. Mistake me not; I repeat that I have never seen you, nor do I wish it; you might be other than I imagine, and I should lose an idol, and be left without a worship. I am a kind of visionary Rosicrucian: it is a spirit that I adore, and not a being like myself. You imagine, perhaps, that I have some purpose to serve in this—I have no object in administering to your vanity; and if I judge you rightly, this letter is one that might make you vain without a blush. Oh, the admiration that does not spring from holy and profound sources of emotion—how it saddens us or disgusts! I have had my share of vulgar homage, and it only makes me feel doubly alone. I am richer than you are—I have youth—I have what they call beauty. And neither riches, youth, nor beauty ever gave me the silent and deep happiness I experience when I think of you. This is a worship that might, I repeat, well make even you vain. Think of these words, I implore you. Be worthy, not of my thoughts, but of the shape in which they represent you: and every ray of glory that surrounds you will brighten my own way, and inspire me with a kindred emulation. Farewell.—I may write to you again, but you will never discover me; and in life I pray that we may never meet!"

CHAPTER V.

"Our list of nobles next let Amri grace."
/Absalom and Achitophel.

"Sine me vacivum tempus ne quod dem mihi Laboris."*—TER.

* Suffer me to employ my spare time in some kind of labour.

"I CAN'T think," said one of a group of young men, loitering by the steps of a clubhouse in St. James's Street—"I can't think what has chanced to Maltravers. Do you observe (as he walks—there—the other side of the way) how much he is altered? He stoops like an old man, and hardly ever lifts his eyes from the ground. He certainly seems sick and sad."

"Writing books, I suppose."

"Or privately married."

"Or growing too rich—rich men are always unhappy beings."

"Ha, Ferrers, how are you?"

"So-so. What's the news?" replied Lumley.

"Rattler pays forfeit."

"O! but in politics?"

"Hang politics—are you turned politician?"

"At my age, what else is there left to do?"

"I thought so, by your hat; all politicians sport odd-looking hats: it is very remarkable, but that is the great symptom of the disease."

"My hat!—/is/ it odd?" said Ferrers, taking off the commodity in question, and seriously regarding it.

"Why, who ever saw such a brim?"

"Glad you think so."

"Why, Ferrers?"

"Because it is a prudent policy in this country to surrender something trifling up to ridicule. If people can abuse your hat or your carriage, or the shape of your nose, or a wart on your chin, they let slip a thousand more important matters. 'Tis the wisdom of the camel-driver, who gives up his gown for the camel to trample on, that he may escape himself."

"How droll you are, Ferrers! Well, I shall turn in, and read the papers; and you—"

"Shall pay my visits and rejoice in my hat."

"Good day to you; by the by, your friend, Maltravers, has just passed, looking thoughtful, and talking to himself. What's the matter with him?"

"Lamenting, perhaps, that he, too, does not wear an odd hat for gentlemen like you to laugh at, and leave the rest of him in peace. Good day."

On went Ferrers, and soon found himself in the Mall of the Park. Here he was joined by Mr. Templeton.

"Well, Lumley," said the latter (and it may be here remarked that Mr.
Templeton now exhibited towards his nephew a greater respect of manner
and tone than he had thought it necessary to observe before)—"well, Lumley, and have you seen Lord Saxingham?"

"I have, sir; and I regret to say—"

"I thought so—I thought it," interrupted Templeton: "no gratitude in public men—no wish, in high place, to honour virtue!"

"Pardon me; Lord Saxingham declares that he should be delighted to forward your views—that no man more deserves a peerage; but that—"

"Oh, yes; always /buts/!"

"But that there are so many claimants at present whom it is impossible to satisfy; and—and—but I feel I ought not to go on."

"Proceed, sir, I beg."

"Why, then, Lord Saxingham is (I must be frank) a man who has a great regard for his own family. Your marriage (a source, my dear uncle, of the greatest gratification to /me/) cuts off the probable chance of your fortune and title, if you acquire the latter, descending to—"

"Yourself!" put in Templeton, drily. "Your relation seems, for the first time, to have discovered how dear your interests are to him."

"For me, individually, sir, my relation does not care a rush—but he cares a great deal for any member of his house being rich and in high station. It increases the range and credit of his connections; and Lord Saxingham is a man whom connections help to keep great. To be plain with you, he will not stir in this business, because he does not see how his kinsman is to be benefited, or his house strengthened."

"Public virtue!" exclaimed Templeton.

"Virtue, my dear uncle, is a female: as long as she is private property, she is excellent; but public virtue, like any other public lady, is a common prostitute."

"Pshaw!" grunted Templeton, who was too much out of humour to read his nephew the lecture he might otherwise have done upon the impropriety of his simile; for Mr. Templeton was one of those men who hold it vicious to talk of vice as existing in the world; he was very much shocked to hear anything called by its proper name.

"Has not Mrs. Templeton some connections that may be useful to you?"

"No, sir!" cried the uncle, in a voice of thunder.

"Sorry to hear it—but we cannot expect all things: you have married for love—you have a happy home, a charming wife—this is better than a title and a fine lady."

"Mr. Lumley Ferrers, you may spare me your consolations. My wife—"

"Loves you dearly, I dare say," said the imperturbable nephew. "She has so much sentiment, is so fond of poetry. Oh, yes, she must love one who has done so much for her."

"Done so much; what do you mean?"

"Why, with your fortune—your station—your just ambition—you, who might have married any one; nay, by remaining unmarried, have conciliated all my interested, selfish relations—hang them—you have married a lady without connections—and what more could you do for her?"

"Pooh, pooh; you don't know all."

Here Templeton stopped short, as if about to say too much, and frowned; then, after a pause, he resumed, "Lumley, I have married, it is true. You may not be my heir, but I will make it up to you—that is, if you deserve my affection."

"My dear unc—"

"Don't interrupt me, I have projects for you. Let our interests be the same. The title may yet descend to you. I may have no male offspring—meanwhile, draw on me to any reasonable amount—young men have expenses—but be prudent, and if you want to get on in the world, never let the world detect you in a scrape. There, leave me now."

"My best, my heartfelt thanks!"

"Hush—sound Lord Saxingham again; I must and will have this bauble—I have set my heart on it." So saying, Templeton waved away his nephew, and musingly pursued his path towards Hyde Park Corner, where his carriage awaited him. As soon as he entered his demesnes, he saw his wife's daughter running across the lawn to greet him. His heart softened; he checked the carriage and descended: he caressed her, he played with her, he laughed as she laughed. No parent could be more fond.

"Lumley Ferrers has talent to do me honour," said he, anxiously, "but his principles seem unstable. However, surely that open manner is the sign of a good heart."

Meanwhile, Ferrers, in high spirits, took his way to Ernest's house. His friend was not at home, but Ferrers never wanted a host's presence in order to be at home himself. Books were round him in abundance, but Ferrers was not one of those who read for amusement. He threw himself into an easy-chair, and began weaving new meshes of ambition and intrigue. At length the door opened, and Maltravers entered.

"Why, Ernest, how ill you are looking!"

"I have not been well, but I am now recovering. As physicians recommend change of air to ordinary patients—so I am about to try change of habit. Active I must be—action is the condition of my being; but I must have done with books from the present. You see me in a new character."

"How?"

"That of a public man—I have entered parliament."

"You astonish me!—I have read the papers this morning. I see not even a vacancy, much less an election."

"It is all managed by the lawyer and the banker. In other words, my seat is a close borough."

"No bore of constituents. I congratulate you, and envy. I wish I were in parliament myself."

"You! I never fancied you bitten by the political mania."

"Political!—no. But it is the most respectable way, with luck, of living on the public. Better than swindling."

"A candid way of viewing the question. But I thought at one time you were half a Benthamite, and that your motto was, 'The greatest happiness of the greatest number.'"

"The greatest number to me is number /one/. I agree with the Pythagoreans—unity is the perfect principle of creation! Seriously, how can you mistake the principles of opinion for the principles of conduct? I am a Benthamite, a benevolist, as a logician—but the moment I leave the closet for the world, I lay aside speculation for others, and act for myself."

"You are, at least, more frank than prudent in these confessions."

"There you are wrong. It is by affecting to be worse than we are that we become popular—and we get credit for being both honest and practical fellows. My uncle's mistake is to be a hypocrite in words: it rarely answers. Be frank in words, and nobody will suspect hypocrisy in your designs."

Maltravers gazed hard at Ferrers—something revolted and displeased his high-wrought Platonism in the easy wisdom of his old friend. But he felt, almost for the first time, that Ferrers was a man to get on in the world—and he sighed; I hope it was for the world's sake.

After a short conversation on indifferent matters, Cleveland was announced; and Ferrers, who could make nothing out of Cleveland, soon withdrew. Ferrers was now becoming an economist in his time.

"My dear Maltravers," said Cleveland, when they were alone, "I am so glad to see you; for, in the first place, I rejoice to find you are extending your career of usefulness."

"Usefulness—ah, let me think so! Life is so uncertain and so short, that we cannot too soon bring the little it can yield into the great commonwealth of the Beautiful or the Honest; and both belong to and make up the Useful. But in politics, and in a highly artificial state, what doubts beset us! what darkness surrounds! If we connive at abuses, we juggle with our own reason and integrity—if we attack them, how much, how fatally we may derange that solemn and conventional ORDER which is the mainspring of the vast machine! How little, too, can one man, whose talents may not be in that coarse road—in that mephitic atmosphere, be enabled to effect!"

"He may effect a vast deal even without eloquence or labour:—he may effect a vast deal, if he can set one example, amidst a crowd of selfish aspirants and heated fanatics, of an honest and dispassionate man. He may effect more, if he may serve among the representatives of that hitherto unrepresented thing—Literature; if he redeem, by an ambition above place and emolument, the character for subservience that court-poets have obtained for letters—if he may prove that speculative knowledge is not disjoined from the practical world, and maintain the dignity of disinterestedness that should belong to learning. But the end of a scientific morality is not to serve others only, but also to perfect and accomplish our individual selves; our own souls are a solemn trust to our own lives. You are about to add to your experience of human motives and active men;

and whatever additional wisdom you acquire will become equally evident and equally useful, no matter whether it be communicated through action or in books. Enough of this, my dear Ernest. I have come to dine with you, and make you accompany me to-night to a house where you will be welcome, and I think interested. Nay, no excuses. I have promised Lord Latimer that he shall make your acquaintance, and he is one of the most eminent men with whom political life will connect you."

And to this change of habits, from the closet to the senate, had Maltravers been induced by a state of health, which, with most men, would have been an excuse for indolence. Indolent he could not be; he had truly said to Ferrers, that "action was the condition of his being." If THOUGHT, with its fever and aching tension, had been too severe a taskmaster on the nerves and brain, the coarse and homely pursuit of practical politics would leave the imagination and intellect in repose, while it would excite the hardier qualities and gifts, which animate without exhausting. So, at least, hoped Maltravers. He remembered the profound saying in one of his favourite German authors, "that to keep the mind and body in perfect health, it is necessary to mix habitually and betimes in the common affairs of men." And the anonymous correspondent;—had her exhortations any influence on his decision? I know not. But when Cleveland left him, Maltravers unlocked his desk, and re-perused the last letter he had received from the Unknown. The /last/ letter!—yes, those epistles had now become frequent.

CHAPTER VI.

* * * * "Le brillant de votre esprit donne un si grand
  eclat a votre teint et a vos yeux, que quoiqu'il semble
  que l'esprit ne doit toucher que les oreilles, il est
  pourtaut certain que la votre eblouit les yeux."*
  /Lettres de Madame de Sevigne/.

* The brilliancy of your wit gives so great a lustre to your complexion and your eyes, that, though it seems that wit should only reach the ears, it is altogether certain that yours dazzles the eyes.

AT Lord Latimer's house were assembled some hundreds of those persons who are rarely found together in London society; for business, politics, and literature draught off the most eminent men, and usually leave to houses that receive the world little better than indolent rank or ostentatious wealth. Even the young men of pleasure turn up their noses at parties now-a-days, and find society a bore. But there are some dozen or two of houses, the owners of which are both apart from and above the fashion, in which a foreigner may see, collected under the same roof, many of the most remarkable men of busy, thoughtful, majestic England. Lord Latimer himself had been a cabinet minister. He retired from public life on pretence of ill-health; but, in reality, because its anxious bustle was not congenial to a gentle and accomplished, but somewhat feeble, mind. With a high reputation and an excellent cook he enjoyed a great popularity, both with his own party and the world in general; and he was the centre of a small, but distinguished circle of acquaintances, who drank Latimer's wine, and quoted Latimer's sayings, and liked Latimer much better, because, not being author or minister, he was not in their way.

Lord Latimer received Maltravers with marked courtesy, and even deference, and invited him to join his own whist-table, which was one of the highest compliments his lordship could pay to his intellect. But when his guest refused the proffered honour, the earl turned him over to the countess, as having become the property of the womankind; and was soon immersed in his aspirations for the odd trick.

Whilst Maltravers was conversing with Lady Latimer, he happened to raise his eyes, and saw opposite to him a young lady of such remarkable beauty, that he could scarcely refrain from an admiring exclamation.—"And who," he asked, recovering himself, "is that lady? It is strange that even I, who go so little into the world, should be compelled to inquire the name of one whose beauty must already have made her celebrated."

"Oh, Lady Florence Lascelles—she came out last year. She is, indeed, most brilliant, yet more so in mind and accomplishments than face. I must be allowed to introduce you."

At this offer, a strange shyness, and as it were reluctant distrust, seized Maltravers—a kind of presentiment of danger and evil. He drew back, and would have made some excuse, but Lady Latimer did not heed his embarrassment, and was already by the side of Lady Florence Lascelles. A moment more, and beckoning to Maltravers, the countess presented him to the lady. As he bowed and seated himself beside his new acquaintance, he could not but observe that her cheeks were suffused with the most lively blushes, and that she received him with a confusion not common even in ladies just brought out, and just introduced to "a lion." He was rather puzzled than flattered by these tokens of an embarrassment, somewhat akin to his own; and the first few sentences of their conversation passed off with a certain awkwardness and reserve. At this moment, to the surprise, perhaps to the relief, of Ernest, they were joined by Lumley Ferrers.

"Ah, Lady Florence, I kiss your hands—I am charmed to find you acquainted with my friend Maltravers."

"And Mr. Ferrers, what makes him so late to-night?" asked the fair Florence, with a sudden ease, which rather startled Maltravers.

"A dull dinner, /voila tout/—I have no other excuse." And Ferrers, sliding into a vacant chair on the other side of Lady Florence, conversed volubly and unceasingly, as if seeking to monopolise her attention.

Ernest had not been so much captivated with the manner of Florence as he had been struck with her beauty, and now, seeing her apparently engaged with another, he rose and quietly moved away. He was soon one of a knot of men who were conversing on the absorbing topics of the day; and as by degrees the exciting subject brought out his natural eloquence and masculine sense, the talkers became listeners, the knot widened into a circle, and he himself was unconsciously the object of general attention and respect.

"And what think you of Mr. Maltravers?" asked Ferrers, carelessly; "does he keep up your expectations?"

Lady Florence had sunk into a reverie, and Ferrers repeated his question.

"He is younger than I imagined him, — and — and — "

"Handsomer, I suppose, you mean."

"No! calmer and less animated."

"He seems animated enough now," said Ferrers; "but your ladylike conversation failed in striking the Promethean spark. 'Lay that flattering unction to your soul.'"

"Ah, you are right — he must have thought me very — "

"Beautiful, no doubt."

"Beautiful! — I hate the word, Lumley. I wish I were not handsome — I might then get some credit for my intellect."

"Humph!" said Ferrers, significantly.

"Oh, you don't think so, sceptic," said Florence, shaking her head with a slight laugh, and an altered manner.

"Does it matter what I think," said Ferrers, with an attempted touch at the sentimental, "when Lord This, and Lord That, and Mr. So-and-so, and Count What-d'ye-call-him, are all making their way to you, to dispossess me of my envied monopoly?"

While Ferrers spoke, several of the scattered loungers grouped around Florence, and the conversation, of which she was the cynosure, became animated and gay. Oh, how brilliant she was, that peerless Florence! — with what petulant and sparkling grace came wit and wisdom, and even genius, from those ruby lips! Even the assured Ferrers felt his subtle intellect as dull and coarse to hers, and shrank with a reluctant apprehension from the arrows of her careless and prodigal repartees. For there was a scorn in the nature of Florence Lascelles which made her wit pain more frequently than it pleased. Educated even to learning—courageous even to a want of feminacy—she delighted to sport with ignorance and pretension, even in the highest places; and the laugh that she excited was like lightning;—no one could divine where next it might fall.

But Florence, though dreaded and unloved, was yet courted, flattered, and the rage. For this there were two reasons: first, she was a coquette, and secondly, she was an heiress.

Thus the talkers in the room were divided into two principal groups, over one of which Maltravers may be said to have presided; over the other, Florence. As the former broke up, Ernest was joined by Cleveland.

"My dear cousin," said Florence, suddenly, and in a whisper, as she turned to Lumley, "your friend is speaking of me—I see it. Go, I implore you, and let me know what he says!"

"The commission is not flattering," said Ferrers, almost sullenly.

"Nay, a commission to gratify a woman's curiosity is ever one of the most flattering embassies with which we can invest an able negotiator."

"Well, I must do your bidding, though I disown the favour." Ferrers moved away, and joined Cleveland and Maltravers.

"She is, indeed, beautiful: so perfect a contour I never beheld: she is the only woman I ever saw in whom the aquiline features seem more classical than even the Greek."

"So, that is your opinion of my fair cousin!" cried Ferrers, "you are caught."

"I wish he were," said Cleveland. "Ernest is now old enough to settle, and there is not a more dazzling prize in England—rich, high-born, lovely, and accomplished."

"And what say you?" asked Lumley, almost impatiently, to Maltravers.

"That I never saw one whom I admire more or could love less,"
replied
Ernest, as he quitted the rooms.

Ferrers looked after him, and muttered to himself; he then re-joined Florence, who presently rose to depart, and taking Lumley's arm, said, "Well, I see my father is looking round for me — and so for once I will forestall him. Come, Lumley, let us join him; I know he wants to see you.

"Well?" said Florence, blushing deeply, and almost breathless, as they crossed the now half-empty apartments.

"Well, my cousin?"

"You provoke me — well, then, what said your friend?"

"That you deserved your reputation of beauty, but that you were not his style. Maltravers is in love, you know."

"In love?"

"Yes, a pretty Frenchwoman! quite romantic — an attachment of some years' standing."

Florence turned away her face, and said no more.

"That's a good fellow, Lumley," said Lord Saxingham; "Florence is never more welcome to my eyes than at half-past one o'clock A.M., when I associate her with thoughts of my natural rest, and my unfortunate carriage-horses. By the by, I wish you would dine with me next Saturday."

"Saturday: unfortunately I am engaged to my uncle."

"Oh! he has behaved handsomely to you?"

"Yes."

"Mrs. Templeton pretty well?"

"I fancy so."

"As ladies wish to be, etc.?" whispered his lordship.

"No, thank Heaven!"

"Well, if the old man could but make you his heir, we might think twice about the title."

"My dear lord, stop! one favour—write me a line to hint that delicately."

"No—no letters; letters always get into the papers."

"But cautiously worded—no danger of publication, on my honour."

"I'll think of it. Good night."